How to make your Felicity wishes

## WISH

With this book comes an extra-special wish for you and your best friend.

Hold the book together at each end and both close your eyes.

Wriggle your noses and think of a number under ten.

Open your eyes, whisper the numbers you thought of to each other.

Add these numbers together. This is your

### Magic Number.

you

best friend

Place your little finger on the stars, and say your magic number out loud together. Now make your wish quietly to yourselves. And maybe, one day, your wish might just come true.

Love felicity x

With extra-special wishes for Grandad and Rene
with love, Emma x

FELICITY WISHES

FELICITY WISHES

Felicity Wishes © 2000 Emma Thomson
Licensed by White Lion Publishing

Text and Illustrations © 2007 Emma Thomson

First published in Great Britain in 2007 by Hodder Children's Books

A Catalogue record for this book is available from the British Library.

ISBN: 9 780 34094392 2

Printed in the UoK by CPI Bookmarque, Croydon, CR0 4TD

Hodder Children's Books
A division of Hachette Children's Books, 338 Euston Road, London NW1 3BH

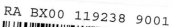

# Crowning Cure

### and other stories

Hodder
Children's
Books

A division of Hachette Children's Books

# CONTENTS

# Crowning Cure

Felicity Wishes and her friends were in their favourite café, Sparkles, after school. They were listening to Winnie as she told them about her adventures on Bubble Island over the weekend.

"There are beautiful lagoons everywhere, with magical bubbles of every colour rising out of them!" Winnie was so excited she could hardly speak fast enough. "One lagoon in the very middle of the island was filled with a foam made of millions of miniature rainbow bubbles that smelt of strawberries!"

"Did you go swimming?" Holly asked.

"Oh no, the water isn't safe. They say that if you swim in it you'll turn into a giant bubble and float into the sky!"

The fairies gasped.

"Has it ever happened to anyone?" Daisy asked worriedly.

"I think that's just one of the island legends. But there are lots of nasty bubbly bugs you can catch if you go too close to the water," Winnie explained.

"Well, I hope you stayed well back," Polly said. "We have an important wish-making exam in a few days."

The fairies groaned. They didn't want to be reminded of the exam Fairy Godmother had set the previous Friday.

"I'll be fine," Winnie told Polly. "I was practising all weekend."

Felicity sank back into her chair. She had been in such a rush to leave school on Friday afternoon and welcome the weekend that she'd completely forgotten to make a note of the exam. She hadn't practised at all.

"What are we going to do with you, Felicity?" Polly said with a sigh, smiling at her forgetful friend.

"It's OK, Felicity, we've got four more days. Plenty of time to practise!" Daisy reassured her.

\* \* \*

Felicity flew into school the next morning with only one thing on her mind. She'd hardly done any practice for the exam, and time was running out. She was so preoccupied with fitting everything in to her busy schedule that she didn't look where she was going. She flew straight into Winnie, who toppled backwards mid-flutter and landed on the ground in a heap.

"I'm so sorry," Felicity exclaimed,

quickly bending down to help Winnie
up. "Are you OK?"

At first Winnie didn't answer, but just
stared straight ahead of her as though
nothing had happened. As Felicity took
her hand, she seemed to come round
from her daze and looked quizzically
at her friend.

"What happened?" she asked,
confused.

"I didn't look where I was going –
I was thinking about the exam – and
I didn't see you…" Felicity's voice
trailed off as she looked at Winnie,

who seemed even more puzzled.

"What exam?" Winnie asked.

"The wish-making exam, remember? Polly reminded us yesterday, and you said you'd been practising all weekend," Felicity reminded Winnie.

"Oh, oh yes, I'd completely forgotten." Winnie stood up and dusted off her skirt. "Where are we?" she said, looking around her.

"We're at school," Felicity replied. By now she was quite worried about her friend.

"But I was at home a minute ago! I don't remember flying here at all," Winnie said with a frown.

"Maybe you were daydreaming the whole way here," Felicity suggested kindly, trying to reassure Winnie. "Sometimes I don't remember what I've done because I'm too busy thinking of something else!"

"Yes, maybe that was it." Unsure of

what had happened, Winnie flew off into the school.

As soon as Felicity saw her other friends, she told them what had happened so that they could all keep an eye out for Winnie. But the next day as Felicity was going into her science lesson, Holly started telling her that exactly the same thing had happened on her way into school that morning. Winnie had flown right into her!

"She didn't remember how she had got to school and she'd forgotten to bring her bag. I had to lend her my spare pen and notebook," Holly explained before Miss Sparkle came into the room and the fairies had to be quiet.

At lunchtime Felicity, Polly, Daisy, Holly and Winnie all met under the Large Oak Tree. They were happily chatting about the latest fashions in *Fairy Girl*, their favourite magazine, when Winnie abruptly stopped talking, mid-sentence. The fairies all looked at her, waiting for her to finish what she was saying, but she just sat staring straight ahead.

"Winnie, hello, Winnie?" Felicity called, waving her hand in front of her friend's face. But Winnie didn't even blink.

"What's wrong with her?" Daisy asked, as Holly started shaking Winnie's shoulder to try to rouse her.

"I don't know, but I think we should get her to the school nurse." Polly took both of Winnie's hands and pulled her to her feet.

With Polly on one side and Felicity on the other, Winnie fluttered across the playground to the nurse's office – but she was still in a dream-like state, her eyes glazed over.

The nurse helped Polly and Felicity to lie Winnie down on the sick bed, then told them to wait outside. After only a few minutes the door opened and Winnie came striding out as though nothing had happened.

"Oh!" Felicity exclaimed, jumping off her chair and rushing up to give Winnie a huge hug. "You're OK!"

"Of course I am. The nurse thinks I'm just overly worried about the exam on Friday and should get more rest. She's given me some lavender oil to help me sleep," Winnie said, holding up a tiny purple bottle.

The other fairies were not convinced, but after all the nurse knew best! They smiled at Winnie and walked with her to their next class.

* * *

The rest of the day passed just as usual.
Winnie seemed fine and stayed fully
conscious throughout her lessons, and
all the fairies went home at the end
of the day to practise for their exam.

But the next morning when Felicity
arrived at school, she couldn't see
Winnie anywhere.

"Polly, have you seen Winnie today?"
Felicity asked as she spotted Polly
through the crowd and fluttered up
to her.

"No! I phoned her this morning to
ask if she'd like to fly to school with
me, but she didn't answer her phone
and I thought she must have come into
school early. I can't find her anywhere,
though," Polly said, eyebrows furrowed
with worry.

"I'm going to find her," Felicity said
with determination, flying off in the

direction of Winnie's house with Polly close behind her.

When they arrived the front door was wide open and Winnie was standing in the doorway, wearing the same glazed expression as the day before.

"Winnie!" Felicity called, rushing up to her.

"Quick, let's get her to the school nurse," Polly said, taking Winnie's arm. Winnie willingly flew the whole way to school with Polly and Felicity holding on to her, but she didn't say a word and didn't even seem to know what was happening. Then, just as the three fairies arrived outside the nurse's office, Winnie suddenly came round from her daze.

She looked at Felicity and Polly in surprise. "What happened?" she asked.

"You went into a daydream again," Felicity replied. "We found you in your house, halfway out of the door."

Winnie frowned, trying to remember what she had been doing.

"Last night," she began, "when I got home I started to practise for the wish-making exam. But before I knew it, it was dark outside and time to go to bed. The evening had just disappeared! I used the lavender oil like the nurse said, rubbing it on to the star on my wand and waving it in the air above my head before I went to sleep – and I felt wonderful this morning; I slept perfectly! Then I thought I would come into school early to practise, and now here I am."

Polly knocked on the nurse's door. "Tell her everything you just told us," she instructed Winnie.

The nurse looked very confused by the time Winnie had finished her story, and scratched her head with her wand as she paced the room. This time Felicity and Polly sat beside Winnie on the sick bed, telling the nurse how they had found Winnie in her doorway.

"It seems as though you are falling into daydreams from which you cannot be woken," the nurse said. "If you are sleeping well, as you've told me, it would suggest it's some kind of virus…" She trailed off thoughtfully.

"It's as though she's in her own little bubble!" Felicity said, jumping off the bed and pacing the room with the nurse.

"Well, of course, the symptoms do resemble those of bubblearia, but that is a very, very rare condition and unless you've been to Bubble Island recently…"

"She has, she has!" Felicity squealed, jumping up and down. "She went last weekend."

"Oh dear!" The nurse shook her head and rushed to the phone. "Ambulance please!" she demanded into the receiver.

Felicity, Polly and Winnie looked at each other in shock as the nurse put the phone down.

"What's happening?" Felicity asked her.

"We must get Winnie to the hospital as soon as possible," the nurse explained. "She must be given the antidote before she has another—" The nurse stopped mid-sentence, looking at Winnie. Once again, Winnie's eyes had glazed over and she was staring into space.

When the ambulance arrived, Felicity and Polly, with Holly and Daisy who had come to find the others, went

with Winnie to the Little Blossoming
District Hospital. Winnie was
immediately rushed off to the <u>rare
illnesses</u> ward.

"She'll be OK, Felicity," Daisy
reassured her friend as she put a
comforting arm around her shoulder.
"The nurses will look after her and
she'll be back to her <u>usual</u> self in no
time."

"I feel so useless," Felicity said as she slumped into a chair. "I want to do something to help!"

"I know what you mean," said Holly, giving her a hug.

Suddenly, Felicity had an idea. She jumped to her feet. "How about we go to Winnie's house and get all her favourite things to surround her with? That will make her feel better!"

"Excellent!" Polly agreed.

For a moment, Felicity was reluctant to leave the hospital. But she knew there was nothing she could do to help, so she set out with her friends for Winnie's house.

✳ ✳ ✳

When the fairies arrived, they searched the house for everything they thought Winnie would want.

"I know I wouldn't want to be without my cuddly dog," Daisy said, picking up Winnie's well-loved giraffe

from her bed and adding him to the
bag they had slowly been filling.

"How about the map of Wing Island?"
Felicity called from downstairs. She
hoped it would bring back lots of
lovely memories from the last holiday
the fairies had gone on together.

"And her lucky shell. We can't forget
that!" Polly called back from Winnie's
sitting room.

When the bag was
full to bursting, the
fairies carried it
to the hospital.
They were told
to wait in the corridor outside Winnie's
room, and after a few minutes a nurse
fluttered out.

"How is she?" Felicity asked, jumping
up.

"She still hasn't come round from
her daze. We've tried everything to
wake her, but each daze lasts longer

and longer as the virus gets worse. She could be like this for days, and we can't give her the antidote until she has woken up."

The fairies all frowned.

"Is there anything we can do to help?" Polly asked.

"Well, I see you've got some of Winnie's personal belongings together," the nurse said, looking at their bulging bag. "That always helps. But there's nothing else you can do."

"Can we see her?" Daisy asked tentatively.

"Oh yes, of course, but only one at a time."

The fairies took it in turns to go in to see Winnie. Felicity waited until last, because she knew she would want to stay with Winnie the longest.

As she entered the room, she gasped. Winnie had never looked so tiny, tucked up under the crisp white hospital sheets. Polly had already placed all Winnie's things around the room, but Winnie was staring straight ahead, her eyes wide open and unblinking.

"Winnie, wake up!" Felicity said, prodding Winnie gently with her wand. But Winnie didn't even move.

"Oh, if only there was something I could do," Felicity said desperately, fluttering around the room.

She picked up the map of Wing Island from the shelf where Polly had placed it.

"Look, Winnie, remember our holiday!" she said, fluttering back to the bed. "Remember Ollie the octogiant, and how hard we had to work on the boat, and how magical the island was!"

But nothing Felicity said seemed to get through to Winnie.

"Winnie, we brought your lucky

shell," Felicity said, picking it up from the bedside table. "We know you wouldn't want to be without it. I know, I'll make you a special pouch to put it in, then you can take it everywhere!"

Still Winnie said nothing.

Eventually, Felicity gave up trying to wake her friend. She lay down on the bed next to her and gave her a big hug, wishing with all her heart that Winnie would wake up.

"Don't squeeze too tight, Felicity, I'll burst!"

Felicity thought she had imagined the tiny voice talking to her – but when she sat up Winnie was smiling, looking straight at her!

"Oh, thank goodness!" Felicity cheered, fluttering swiftly to the door. "I'll get the nurse!"

Within seconds the room was filled with fairies. Two nurses gave Winnie the antidote she needed: Winnie had to stand on one leg, jump up and down, twirl to the left three times, then to the right three times, and at the same time take a spoonful of bubbly, multicoloured medicine!

Holly, Polly, Felicity and Daisy were all sitting at the end of Winnie's bed, because there was no room left to stand! A senior nurse came to ask Felicity how she had woken Winnie.

"I didn't do anything!" Felicity told her. "I just gave her a hug and wished very hard, and all of a sudden she woke up."

"It's extremely rare to find a fairy with a natural talent like yours," said the nurse. "How would you like to help out around the hospital for a little while?"

Felicity beamed the biggest smile and said yes before the nurse had even finished her sentence. "It will have to be after school and at the weekends, though. And I can't for the next few days; I've got an exam to practise for!" Felicity said, remembering her wish-making exam.

"Then start this weekend," the nurse

suggested. She turned to Winnie. "And you should be getting back into bed. There won't be any exams for you this week!"

Winnie smiled and did as she was told, while Felicity rushed over to plump the pillows and tuck in the sheets. As Winnie lay down to sleep Felicity gave her another big hug. She knew that a friendly face was the best medicine of all!

A smile can brighten up

even the greyest day

# Medicine Mix-up

Felicity Wishes was on her way to the Little Blossoming District Hospital. She couldn't become a nurse until she had graduated from the School of Nine Wishes, but she'd been offered the opportunity to care for patients after school and at the weekends.

"Right, Felicity, I'm Nurse Florrie Sparrow." A very organized-looking nurse welcomed Felicity at the main entrance. She began to tell her all about the hospital as they fluttered together down long corridors.

"We're going to start with apparently simple jobs," Nurse Florrie continued, "but there are certain ways to do things in a hospital, which I'm going to show you." She came to a stop outside the rare illnesses ward, where Winnie was still a patient.

"I am told by my nursing staff you have a natural talent for caring, so I'm sure you'll pick everything up in no time."

Felicity beamed, hoping she could live up to her reputation.

"As your friend is already on this ward, we shall start with her. Follow me!"

Winnie was in hospital recovering from bubblearia, a rare disease she'd caught on Bubble Island. Felicity had visited her so much she'd made friends with all the fairies on Winnie's ward.

Letty had crumpled-wing syndrome, from too much hugging. Pippa had twinkly-toeitis from too much dancing. Alice had a floppy-wrist condition from a faulty wand. Megan had turned bright yellow after drinking too many banana milkshakes. And Tabitha had flown into a tree while daydreaming and had temporary memory loss from banging her head. They all waved at Felicity as she fluttered past.

"Firstly we shall plump Winnie's pillows. Lean forward, please!" Nurse Florrie said to Winnie as she bent over her bed.

"That's easy. I've done that over and over again!" Felicity thought to herself.

"First you must take the pillow off the bed and hold it above your head as you jump up and down five times," said the nurse. "Then you must turn once to the left and twice to the right, shake the pillow three times behind you and finally hold the pillow in front of you as though giving it a hug."

Felicity tried very hard not to giggle as she watched the nurse. She had never done it like that before!

"Your turn!" Florrie said, handing Felicity the pillow.

"So it's, erm, jump up and down three times, then turn to the right twice, and once to the left, then shake it behind you and give it a hug!"

36

Felicity said with a smile, pleased she had remembered what to do.

"Not quite," Florrie told Felicity, showing her all over again.

By her fifth try, Felicity had perfected the process and Winnie lay back, sighing with content as she sank into her fluffy pillows.

Next, Florrie showed Felicity how to make a bed, tucking each corner in at a precise angle and turning back the sheets to an exact measurement. Then they washed the floor with an extra-special sparkly washing liquid, scrubbing each tile three times in one direction, then three times in the other, once clockwise and twice anti-clockwise. Felicity had never imagined that everything was done so precisely.

At the end of the morning, Nurse Sparrow sent Felicity off on her break.

"When you get back, we will begin administering medicines," she told

Felicity. "It's not as easy as the work we've done so far!"

If it was any more difficult, Felicity thought, there was no way she would be able to remember – she was already having trouble!

\* \* \*

Nurse Florrie met Felicity that afternoon with a list of the fairies they had to treat.

"This is Connie; she has been suffering with double vision. Now, you must shake the bottle twice," Florrie said, taking Connie's medicine out of a cupboard, "then put two drops on a spoon, shake the bottle four more times, put one more drop on the spoon, then give it to Connie while she keeps one eye open and one closed."

The afternoon continued: Florrie gave Felicity instructions, and Felicity kept hoping that she would be able to remember them.

"The best thing to do is write down everything we've done today as soon as you get home, before you have the chance to forget! And if you have any worries, just ask me or get any of the nurses to show you their handbook," Nurse Florrie told Felicity when they had finished their day's work. But by the time Felicity got home she was ready to collapse in a heap and barely made it to her bed before falling fast asleep.

\* \* \*

"Good morning, Felicity, I hope you've had a hearty breakfast! You'll need extra energy today!" Nurse Sparrow said when she met Felicity by the hospital entrance the next day. Felicity blushed and hoped the nurse wouldn't hear her tummy grumbling. She hadn't had time for breakfast!

"Firstly you are to revisit all the fairies you saw yesterday," Florrie began, "give them all their medicine, then report back to me. Your friend Winnie will be discharged today, and you can participate in her final assessment before you leave."

Felicity smiled. She knew Winnie couldn't wait to leave – there simply weren't enough adventures to be had along the boring hospital corridors!

"Don't forget," Florrie finished, "you must give the medicines in the exact way I showed you or they might not have the full effect."

Felicity fluttered off to her first ward.

"Hello and hello!" Connie said as Felicity landed beside her bed.

"I think it's, erm, four drops, then

shake it once, then another two drops and take it with one eye open!" Felicity thought to herself, giving the spoon to Connie in the hope she'd got it right.

Felicity visited every patient and spent plenty of time with each, until her head ached with trying to remember what to do.

The afternoon passed much more smoothly. Florrie and Felicity checked Winnie over, making sure she was well enough to go home.

"I'm giving you a week's supply of medicine. You must mix it in a glass with water," Florrie instructed Winnie, "then, using a straw, blow bubbles into the mixture for a minute, then take a sip while closing your eyes and shaking your head, then drink the rest in one go with both eyes open and your left arm behind your back. I'm sure Felicity will be able to remind you of all that if you forget!"

Felicity and Winnie left the hospital together.

"The trouble is, I can't quite remember how to give all the medicines!" Felicity said worriedly to her friend.

"I'm sure you did fine, Felicity!" Winnie reassured her.

"But I can't even remember how you have to take yours," Felicity said desperately, "and Nurse Florrie only told us two minutes ago!"

Winnie gave her friend a big hug. "I'm sure it doesn't matter if you change it a little bit."

Felicity hoped Winnie was right.

\* \* \*

For the next few weeks, Felicity continued working at the hospital after school and at the weekends. She loved making new friends, but she was always sad to see them go, and everyone she treated seemed to get better so quickly! Even Connie had completely recovered and gone home.

All the fairies who had been on Winnie's ward had left, after thanking Felicity for caring for them so well. Felicity had visited Letty twice each day, gently smoothing her wings with her hands until all the crumples had disappeared. She had made Pippa special dance shoes with dandelion down woven into

the toes for extra
cushioning. She
had created a wrist
support for Alice
from an old pair
of stripy tights, and

had brought Megan samples of every
flavour of milkshake to show her that
there were lots of lovely
flavours besides
banana.

Finally, she had made Tabitha a
beautiful notebook to write down

everything she thought she might forget.

* * *

"Ah, Felicity, I'm glad I've found you," Nurse Florrie said, bumping into Felicity as she arrived at the hospital one morning. "I have several fairies training to be nurses and I'd love you to show them round the wards. They all have handbooks on medicine administration, but I'd like you to show them exactly how to do it. I'll fetch them immediately." And with that Florrie flew off, leaving a bewildered Felicity.

Seconds later, Florrie returned with a trail of fairies behind her.

"Follow Felicity, and she will show you all what to do," Florrie said, turning to flutter away.

"Right, erm, OK," Felicity began, unsure what to say to the sea of expectant faces before her. "I usually start with the broken bones and wings ward, because they are the quickest to treat. Follow me!" She spun around and headed off.

"This is Hatty," Felicity said to the fairies as she stopped by the first bed on the ward. "She fell on her head while doing a triple loop-the-loop, and her crown got stuck on to her head."

Hatty smiled when she saw Felicity. "Hatty's bandage needs changing every day," Felicity continued, as Hatty leant forward in bed and Felicity removed the bandage already on her head. "The crown needs to be moved gently back and forth twelve times, three times a day. Then the new dressing must be soaked in warm water for ten seconds. Place a protective layer of cotton around the head first, then smooth the bandage on to her crown by running your hands over each layer six times until you have completed the four layers."

Felicity smiled at the fairies all crammed at the end of the bed, peering over each other's shoulders. She noticed that a couple of the fairies were frowning, but guessed they were probably just trying to remember exactly what she had done.

Next, Felicity took them to the magical mistakes ward, where she treated Carrie, who had added too much sparkledust to a science experiment at school and had ended up sparkling from head to toe!

"Carrie has to take de-sparkling medicine, which must be given using a wooden spoon," Felicity began. "You must shake the bottle six times to your right and five to your left, then put four drops on the spoon, wait three seconds, add another two, then Carrie must take it while holding her nose and tipping her head to the left." Carrie took the medicine as Felicity had instructed. Once again, Felicity noticed some of the fairies were frowning, and a few had started to flick through their handbooks.

"Excuse me," said a very little voice from the front of the crowd. "It says in our instructions that de-sparkling medicine must only be given with a metal spoon, and that you should shake the bottle six times to your left then five to your right, then put three drops on the spoon, wait four seconds then add another two."

Felicity blushed and looked at Carrie.

"Well, I think Felicity's done a great job, and my sparkle has been fading anyway," Carrie said. "When I came in, everyone had to wear sunglasses just to look at me!"

Felicity smiled appreciatively and moved on to her next patient.

"You have to jump up and down and twirl the bottle in your hands seven times, before squeezing seven drops on to a spoon, then wait for six seconds before adding another five," Felicity said confidently.

"No, it's shake the bottle then twirl your arm as you put five drops on the spoon, wait six seconds and add another seven," called a fairy from the back of the group.

"Oh, erm, thank you," Felicity said, blushing again.

By the time Felicity had finished visiting each ward, the fairies had told her she'd been giving every medicine incorrectly.

"What am I going to do?" she said to Holly, Polly, Winnie and Daisy in Sparkles café that evening. "I've been doing it all wrong!"

"Well, no one has got any worse since you've been seeing them, have they?" Winnie asked.

"I don't think so." Felicity hadn't been told that anyone had got worse – but then, so many of her patients had gone home already.

"I'm sure it will be OK, Felicity. Nurse Florrie wouldn't have asked you to do it if there was the chance that you'd make someone worse," Daisy comforted her.

"But you really should tell Nurse

Florrie, just in case," Polly said.

"I know," Felicity agreed. "I just feel awful."

But with the help of her friends, Felicity decided to go to Nurse Florrie first thing the next day and tell her everything.

* * *

"So you see, I just couldn't remember, and now it turns out I've been doing it wrong all along," Felicity finished.

"I see. Well, thank you for coming to tell me, Felicity. I've heard nothing but good reports of your time here!" reassured Nurse Florrie. "But there will of course have to be an investigation, and we will let you know the outcome before the end of the day." She showed Felicity to her office door.

Felicity didn't stop worrying all day, and stuck to the cleaning jobs she'd been shown when she first started.

Just as she was fluttering down the

corridor to leave, she bumped into
Nurse Florrie, accompanied by a very
official-looking fairy in an entirely
white outfit with a green cross on her
front. Even her wings were white with
green crosses at the tips!

"Felicity, we've been looking for
you," Florrie said.

Felicity gulped, her wings quivering.

WARDS
3-5

WARD
6

"There has been a full investigation regarding the information you gave me this morning. The files of each patient you've treated have been examined and their progress reports analysed. There does appear to be a significant difference in the recovery rates from those we would normally expect."

Felicity was ready to burst into tears. "I'm so sorry," she began. "I just—"

But Florrie interrupted her. "The patients you treated have recovered much faster than we've ever seen – in fact, some have had simply miraculous results!"

Felicity couldn't believe it. "So it doesn't matter that I got all their medicines wrong?" she asked hesitantly.

"The most important thing is not the details of how you provide the medicine, but the care and love you put into giving it. Supervising Nurse Carmella here has come to congratulate

you on your magical work and ask you
to give the nursing staff at the hospital
a demonstration of your wonderful
care," Nurse Florrie said, giving Felicity
a hug. "You are the most naturally
friendly and caring fairy we have ever
come across in this hospital, and you
would make a wonderful Carer Fairy."

Felicity beamed. She was so pleased
that she'd been able to help all those
fairies get better. And she couldn't
wait to tell her friends!

Look after your friends
and they will
look after you

# Super Strength

Felicity Wishes was working at the Little Blossoming District Hospital, caring for patients after school and at the weekends. She loved her job making new friends and helping them to get better, but it also made her a little sad.

"I make a new friend, and then the next day she goes home!" Felicity said to Winnie, Holly, Polly and Daisy at school one day.

"It means you're doing your job brilliantly," Daisy told her.

"I'd just like to do something a bit different," Felicity said, imagining working in the fairy surgery or checking fairies in at reception. "After all, I'm only going to be there another week."

"Speak to Nurse Sparrow! You never know, there might be something else you can do," Polly suggested.

Felicity asked Nurse Florrie Sparrow first thing the next day.

"Well, as it happens, I was going to ask you if you wanted to help in the ambulance," Nurse Florrie replied. "Ambulance number 3542 is one crew member down and they need someone to help. It will be similar to the work you have been doing in the hospital – fetching, carrying, general caring. What do you think?"

"I'd love to!" Felicity was thrilled. Going in an ambulance sounded very exciting.

"Excellent," said Nurse Florrie. "You just need to go and fetch a uniform from the washing room. Go straight down the corridor and turn left at the end, then take the third door on the right, go up the stairs, go along the corridor and take the second door on the left, then turn right twice, go down the stairs and take the middle door ahead of you."

Felicity did as Florrie had said… or, at least, she tried to.

"So it's left at the end, third door on the right, up the stairs, third door on left, turn left twice, down the stairs, oh…"

Felicity had been doing her best to remember the way – but she was definitely lost and there were no fairies in sight to ask for directions.

"Perhaps if I go back the way I came," she thought, "I could start again, or find someone to ask." But she only seemed to get more and more lost the further she went, and still there was no one in sight.

Felicity kept fluttering down corridors she had never seen before. She sighed in desperation. Taking another left turn, she found herself in a dark corridor with no windows and only one door at the very end. She went up to it and tried to peer in, but there was something stuck across the window on the other side of the door and she couldn't see anything.

Felicity wondered what could be in this mysterious room; there was no name plate on the door, or ward name swinging above her head. Perhaps if she just had a quick look…

Felicity inched the door open and stepped inside. Immediately lights flickered on above her head, flooding the room in a yellow glow and making Felicity nearly jump out of her wings.

"Oh!" she exclaimed, looking at a tall box standing in the middle of the room. "What in Fairy World is that?" And she tiptoed closer.

It looked a bit like one of the old-fashioned telephone boxes Felicity had seen in her history textbook, but it was round and had all sorts of buttons on the outside. It was made from shiny silver metal that reflected Felicity like a mirror, except for one place where there was a great big glass window the full height of the box.

Next to the window there was a doorway. Felicity nearly dropped her wand when it slowly started opening. There was someone inside!

Out stepped a tall, beautiful fairy
dressed all in green.

"Greetings, Felicity Wishes!" she said in a low voice. "Yes," she continued, noticing Felicity's look of surprise, "your name has come to my attention because you've helped so many fairies get better over the last few weeks. I have come to give you a special gift, which will let you help even more fairies. But it will last a short time only – so make the most of it!"

Felicity couldn't speak. Nothing like this had ever happened to her before. But she immediately trusted the fairy in green, and couldn't wait to find out more about the machine.

"Come and have a look around!" gestured the fairy. Felicity was intrigued; as she stepped inside she saw all sorts of buttons, levers and flashing lights.

The door slid shut and the capsule started wobbling. Before Felicity knew what was happening, pink beams shot

out from all around them and covered them in a warm pink glow. It was as though someone had wrapped her in a big blanket!

When the machine stopped wobbling, Felicity felt bursting with energy.

"Go well," said the beautiful fairy in green, "and take my best wishes with you!"

Felicity waved goodbye to the strange fairy and jumped out into the room. She fluttered as fast as she could along each corridor, and in what seemed like no time at all she was standing outside a door labelled Washing Room.

She found a uniform and sped back to find Florrie, knowing she had been gone ages.

"Oops!" At the end of the next corridor, Felicity caught sight of Florrie slipping on a freshly polished floor. Felicity rushed up to help her and caught her in mid-air – just in time!

"Oh, thank you," Florrie said, steadying herself. "You must have flown at super-speed to reach me!"

"I've just got so much energy!"
Felicity called, doing a loop-the-loop.
She decided it was best not to tell the
nurse about her little adventure.

"Well, you're needed on ward five
to help move a bed, and then you are
to join the ambulance crew."

Felicity sped away, arriving on the
ward seconds later. Several fairies were
crowded around a bed, puffing and
panting.

"Oh good, we need an extra pair of
hands," said one of the fairies, noticing
Felicity. "We're trying to move this bed
over to the window."

Felicity zoomed up to the bed and
moved it all on her own! The other
fairies stood around her, their mouths
hanging open in shock.

"It usually takes six fairies to move
a bed," gasped one of them.

Felicity smiled. "I'm feeling very
energetic!" And with that she rushed

off to join the ambulance crew.

Once there, she was given a thorough tour of the ambulance and shown exactly what she had to do by Lucy, the fairy in charge.

"Mainly you will be following our instructions," Lucy told her, "fetching things as we need them and helping to carry injured fairies."

As it turned out, there were no calls for the ambulance that day. Although Felicity felt a little disappointed, she flew home much more quickly than usual. It only took her a few seconds, compared to her normal ten minutes!

"I've got so much energy!" Felicity thought to herself, reaching her front door. "I wonder…"

She flew up to her bedroom and looked at her bed. Whenever she'd wanted to rearrange her room before, she'd had to ask all her friends to help her. But since she could lift the bed in the hospital…

Grabbing the end of the bed, she lifted it above her head. It felt as light as a feather! Next she moved her wardrobe, desk and drawers, putting them all in new places. Then she started on her

guest bedroom and before she knew it she had completely rearranged her whole house!

Just then the doorbell rang. Felicity answered it to find Daisy, Holly, Polly and Winnie all standing on her doorstep.

"We came to see how it went today," Daisy began, peering over Felicity's shoulder. "But it looks as though you've been busy!"

Felicity let all the fairies in, then started twirling her sofa above her head!

Her friends stood there in shock, their eyes as wide as moons! Felicity made them all hot chocolates, extra quickly, and sat down to tell them everything that had happened.

"So this machine has given you super-strength?" Polly asked shakily.

"Yes, I think so!" Felicity replied, twisting her teaspoon into a knot.

"Wow." Holly still couldn't believe Felicity had rearranged the house all by herself.

"What are you going to do now?" Daisy asked.

"Well, I already love being at the hospital. I'd really like to put my powers to use and do more to help."

"Yes but once you show other fairies what you can do, they'll all want you to help them, and you won't have enough time at the hospital," Polly said.

"I know!" Holly squealed, jumping up from the sofa. "You need a disguise!" She rushed upstairs and started tearing through Felicity's wardrobe.

"I've got an old pair of stripy tights, and some pink sparkly material!" Holly said as she rushed out of the door.

Hours later the fairies had all started to yawn with tiredness – except Felicity, who was still wide awake. Holly reappeared with a bag in her hand.

"Here!" she said, handing it to Felicity. "Try it on!"

Inside was a mass of pink material; Felicity shook it out and put it on. Holly had made a tight knee-length dress, cut on a slant at the bottom. One arm had a long sleeve, and the other was sleeveless. From Felicity's old tights, Holly had made a belt and a stripy sleeve to put over Felicity's bare arm. A long billowing cape tied

around Felicity's neck, embroidered with a huge white "SF". Finally, there was a stripy mask with two slits cut for her eyes.

"I love it!" Felicity said, zooming around the room in a pink blur. "SuperFairy, here to help you!"

The next day Felicity took her uniform to work with her in a bag.

"What have you got there?" Lucy asked as Felicity arrived at the ambulance station.

"Oh, nothing, just a few things I need," Felicity said carefully.

Within seconds, the ambulance was called to its first emergency of the day.

"A hiker is trapped in a hole beneath two fallen rocks at the bottom of a mountain," crackled Lucy's walkie-talkie.

As soon as they arrived at the scene, Felicity hid behind a rock and changed into her costume.

None of the fairies knew what was happening as a pink blur zoomed up to the fallen rocks and started to lift them away, releasing the trapped fairy.

"But they couldn't... We tried... Ten of us... Wouldn't move," one fairy stuttered.

Felicity's work done, she zoomed away again and got changed back into her ambulance uniform.

"Oh, Felicity, where were you? You just missed the most amazing thing!" Lucy said as Felicity appeared by her side. She went on to tell Felicity the whole story, while Felicity asked lots of questions, as if she didn't know what had happened.

The next day after school, Felicity went to join the ambulance crew again. This time they were called to a fairy who had hurt her leg falling off a swing in the park.

"She needs to get to hospital as quickly as possible – the leg needs setting in plaster immediately," Lucy told Felicity as she examined the injured fairy. Once again Felicity disappeared, this time behind some trees, and reappeared in seconds as SuperFairy. She lifted the fairy off the

ground and flew her to the
hospital in a flash.

This time, many
more fairies
saw Felicity –
and by the
next morning
a sketched
picture of
SuperFairy
was on the
front page of

every newspaper with the headline:
"SuperFairy Saves the Day!"

Everyone was talking about it as
Felicity arrived at school.

That afternoon, the ambulance got
stuck in a traffic jam as it was taking
a casualty back to hospital. Felicity
quickly changed behind a post box
and lifted the ambulance into the air,
flying it all the way to the front of the
queue!

"You're so unlucky," Lucy said as Felicity got back in the ambulance. "You've never seen SuperFairy – you've never been here when she's appeared."

* * *

Felicity hadn't needed to sleep since she had been turned into SuperFairy. But that night, as the sun set over the hills in Little Blossoming, she started to feel tired. She went to bed worrying that Lucy might have guessed her secret, but fell into a deep sleep as soon as her head hit the pillow.

* * *

The next morning Felicity woke feeling refreshed and ready to face the day. She decided she'd move her table outside so she could have breakfast in the garden. But no matter how hard she tried, it just wouldn't budge!

Hoping that she was just taking time to get her strength back, she fluttered off to school. Since she'd been able to fly at super-speed, she'd been setting her alarm clock only ten minutes before the first school bell. But today she arrived twenty minutes late, puffing from trying to fly as fast as she possibly could.

At lunchtime she told her friends what had happened.

"So it's completely worn off?" Daisy asked.

Felicity nodded.

"You can't do anything special any more?" Polly asked.

Felicity shook her head.

"Well, there's only one thing for it, you have to find that capsule again!" Winnie told her.

But Felicity had been thinking about this all day.

"It's nice to have super powers," she told her friends, "but it's ever so tiring and I'm sure Lucy was about to guess that SuperFairy was me. I just want to be normal and go to Sparkles with you after school!"

Felicity's friends smiled. They had all missed having her around.

"Don't worry, Felicity!" Polly reassured her. "You can do just as much good to other fairies with your care and friendship as you can being SuperFairy!"

Felicity nodded. Then, out of the corner of her eye, she caught a glimpse of something shiny out of the window. She was almost sure that it was the fairy in green, smiling and waving at her as she flew away in her sparkling machine.

Emma Thomson's
Felicity Wishes

Felicity and her friends

explore an old mansion

full of history in

Fairy Fame

# Mystery Mansion

Felicity Wishes and her friends were sitting in Sparkles, their favourite café, trying to decide what to do. It was the first Saturday in ages that none of them had any plans.

"We could go bowling," Holly suggested.

"I went last weekend," Winnie said.

"How about ice-skating?" Felicity proposed. But Polly had heard it was shut for repairs.

"We could go for a walk in the woods," Daisy said dreamily.

"I've lost my walking boots," Felicity replied.

None of the fairies knew what to do.

"Unless…" Winnie began, then paused.

"What?" they all chorused.

"Well, ever since I came to Little Blossoming I've wanted to explore the old mansion over the hill," Winnie told them.

Winnie was talking about an old ruin of a house on the very outskirts of Little Blossoming. The fairies had flown over it hundreds of times but never thought about going inside.

"That old thing! Why would you want to go there?" Holly asked, wrinkling her nose.

"It might be fun!" Winnie replied with an adventurous heart.

Felicity smiled. "I don't see why not. It sounds exciting!"

"Wouldn't it be trespassing?" Polly asked sensibly.

"I don't think so. It's abandoned!" Winnie was almost at the door already.

"Then let's go!" Felicity cried, jumping up from her seat.

"At least we'll be outside in the sunshine," Daisy said, following.

Holly and Polly were far more reluctant to go, but without anything better to do they followed their friends.

It didn't take the fairies long to reach the old house; it was far closer than they had thought. Once they got there, though, they found the ancient metal gates closed and locked.

"Well, that's the end of that," Felicity sighed, turning to go home. "We clearly aren't supposed to go in."

"Ta da!" Winnie had been fiddling with the padlock and now the gates swung wide open.

"What did you do?" Holly asked, amazed.

"Magic!" Winnie laughed. "Well, actually the lock had completely rusted through so it just fell apart in my hand. No one has touched it for years. It must be all right to explore."

The fairies cautiously stepped forward into the most overgrown garden they had ever seen.

"Oh, it's so sad," Daisy said, looking at the ivy and brambles covering everything in sight.

They had to flutter above the ground to avoid getting scratched. When they reached the house, the front door was barely visible behind a blanket of creeping ivy and wild roses. Winnie pulled back as much as she could, discovering that the heavy old door was already wedged open. She led the way inside to a very dark and dusty hallway.

"Wow! It's huge!" Felicity said, marvelling at the high ceiling and grand staircase in front of her.

"This room alone is bigger than my house!" Daisy said in amazement.

Holly, meanwhile, had wiped the dust and dirt off a wall with her finger to find some beautiful wallpaper with a bright-blue background and gold swirls beneath. "This must have been such a lovely home," she said, sad that it had become so neglected.

"Come on, let's look around," Winnie said, racing up to the staircase. "Oops! Mind the missing step!"

Upstairs were ten bedrooms, all with four-poster beds covered in dust sheets. Felicity picked up the corner of a sheet to peer underneath, only to find a huge spider!

"Ahhh!" she screamed, jumping back straight into Polly. Polly toppled on to the floor, sending a cloud of dust into the air as she hit the thick rug covering the wooden floorboards.

As Polly got up she saw an intricate pattern of rich colours on the rug where she had unsettled the dust.

"You know, all this needs is a good clean and some tender loving care. I bet it could look as good as new in no time!" she said, looking at the fairies around her.

They all grinned at her, ready to start work straight away!

* * *

The fairies met at eight o'clock the next morning armed with brushes and vacuum cleaners, dusters and polish, floor cleaners, buckets and mops, eager to return to their house. But when they got there the front door was swinging open in the breeze.

"That's funny," Winnie said. "I thought I closed it when we left last night."

They went inside, only to find a fairy sitting on the stairs in the hall.

"Oh, sorry, we, er, thought this place

was deserted," Felicity muttered, feeling very guilty.

"It is!" the fairy replied in a very squeaky voice, almost a whisper. "I just keep an eye on it and I noticed you all here yesterday. I wanted to say hello because I used to live here."

"We're so sorry. We didn't mean to intrude," Polly said, stepping forward. "We didn't think anyone had lived here for years and we wanted to do it up a bit. We'll go!"

"Oh no, please don't!" the fairy squeaked, looking very disappointed. "I lived here a very long time ago, but it was just too big to look after all on my own. I'd love to help you clean it. I can even tell you what it used to look like!"

Felicity smiled. "It would be wonderful to have your help. I'm Felicity and these are my friends Holly, Polly, Winnie and Daisy," she said, introducing everyone.

"I'm Eliza. It's lovely to meet you all," the squeaky fairy smiled.

As Felicity, Holly, Polly and Eliza cleaned the inside of the house, Daisy and Winnie explored the garden.

"You know, with a good pair of shears and a spade I bet this garden could look great in no time!" Daisy said as she fluttered around.

The fairies worked tirelessly all day and well into the night, by candlelight.

Read the rest of

*Emma Thomson's*

# Felicity Wishes
## fairy fame

to find out if the fairies manage

to transform the mansion.

If you enjoyed this book, why not try another of these fantastic story collections?

Designer Drama

Star Surprise

Clutter Clean-out

Newspaper Nerves

Enchanted Escape

Whispering Wishes

**7** Sensational Secrets

**8** Friends Forever

**9** Happy Hobbies

**10** Party Pickle

**11** Wand Wishes

**12** Dancing Dreams

Spooky Sleepover

Fashion Fiasco

Pink Paradise

Spectacular Skies

Dreamy Daisy

Perfect Polly

Winnie's Wonderland

Holly's Hideaway

Fairy Fun

Starlight Songs

Crowning Cure

Fairy Fame

25 — Perfect Ponies

26 — Storytelling Stars

27 — Glittering Giveaways

Look out for these five special editions

Summer Sunshine

Holiday Hullabaloo

Christmas Calamity

Winter Wishes

Snowy Showdown

# SEE YOUR FRIENDSHIP LETTER HERE!

Write in and tell us all about your best friend, and you could see your letter published in one of the Felicity Wishes books.

Please send in your letter, including your name and age, with a stamped self-addressed envelope to:

Felicity Wishes Friendship Competition

Hodder Children's Books, 338 Euston Road, London NW1 3BH

Australian readers should write to...
**Hachette Children's Books**
Level 17/207 Kent Street, Sydney, NSW 2000, Australia

New Zealand readers should write to...
**Hachette Children's Books**
PO Box 100-749 North Shore Mail Centre, Auckland, New Zealand

## Closing date is 31st December 2007

ALL ENTRIES MUST BE SIGNED BY A PARENT OR GUARDIAN.
TO BE ELIGIBLE ENTRANTS MUST BE UNDER 13 YEARS.

For full terms and conditions visit www.felicitywishes.net/terms